Marx Joyce Austen
Defoe Abbott Hardy Machiavelli Chesterton Cooper Emerson Hugo Grimm
Melville Montaigne Haggard Eliot
Carroll Christie Molière
Stoker Maupassant Byron Schiller
Wilde Engels
Garnett Einstein Fitzgerald Hawthorne Smith Kafka Hall
Goethe Kipling Doyle Willis
Cotton Dostoyevsky
Baum Henry Nietzsche
Leslie Dumas Flaubert Turgenev Balzac
Stockton Vatsyayana Crane
Burroughs Verne
Curtis Tocqueville Gogol Vinci
Homer Widger Tolstoy Whitman Busch
Darwin Thoreau Twain
Potter Freud Zola Lawrence Plato Scott
Kant Jowett Stevenson Dickens Burton Hesse Harte
Andersen Cervantes
London Descartes Voltaire
Poe Aristotle Wells
Hale James Hastings Cooke
Bunner Shakespeare Irving
Richter Chambers
Doré da Shaw Wodehouse Benedict Alcott
Dante Chekhov Pushkin
Swift Newton

 tredition®

tredition was established in 2006 by Sandra Latusseck and Soenke Schulz. Based in Hamburg, Germany, tredition offers publishing solutions to authors and publishing houses, combined with world-wide distribution of printed and digital book content. tredition is uniquely positioned to enable authors and publishing houses to create books on their own terms and without conventional manu-facturing risks.

For more information please visit: www.tredition.com

TREDITION CLASSICS

This book is part of the TREDITION CLASSICS series. The creators of this series are united by passion for literature and driven by the intention of making all public domain books available in printed format again - worldwide. Most TREDITION CLASSICS titles have been out of print and off the bookstore shelves for decades. At tredi-tion we believe that a great book never goes out of style and that its value is eternal. Several mostly non-profit literature projects pro-vide content to tredition. To support their good work, tredition donates a portion of the proceeds from each sold copy. As a reader of a TREDITION CLASSICS book, you support our mission to save many of the amazing works of world literature from oblivion. See all available books at www.tredition.com.

Project Gutenberg

The content for this book has been graciously provided by Project Gutenberg. Project Gutenberg is a non-profit organization founded by Michael Hart in 1971 at the University of Illinois. The mission of Project Gutenberg is simple: To encourage the creation and distribu-tion of eBooks. Project Gutenberg is the first and largest collection of public domain eBooks.

Pelham

Volume 8

Baron Edward Bulwer Lytton Lytton

Imprint

This book is part of TREDITION CLASSICS

Author: Baron Edward Bulwer Lytton Lytton
Cover design: Buchgut, Berlin – Germany

Publisher: tredition GmbH, Hamburg - Germany
ISBN: 978-3-8424-3067-9

www.tredition.com
www.tredition.de

VOLUME VIII.

CHAPTER LXXX.

> K. Henry. Lord Say, Jack Cade hath sworn to have thy head.
>
> Say. Ay, but I hope your Highness shall
> have his. —2nd Part of Henry IV.

Punctual to his appointment, the next morning came Mr. Job Jonson. I had been on the rack of expectation for the last three hours previous to his arrival, and the warmth of my welcome must have removed any little diffidence with which so shame-faced a gentleman might possibly have been troubled.

At my request, he sat himself down, and seeing that my breakfast things were on the table, remarked what a famous appetite the fresh air always gave him. I took the hint, and pushed the rolls towards him. He immediately fell to work, and for the next quarter of an hour, his mouth was far too well occupied for the intrusive impertinence of words. At last the things were removed, and Mr. Jonson began.

"I have thought well over the matter, your honour, and I believe we can manage to trounce the rascals—for I agree with you, that there is not a doubt that Thornton and Dawson are the real criminals; but the affair, Sir, is one of the greatest difficulty and importance—nay, of the greatest personal danger. My life may be the forfeit of my desire to serve you—you will not, therefore, be surprised at my accepting your liberal offer of three hundred a year, should I be successful; although I do assure you, Sir, that it was my original intention to reject all recompence, for I am naturally benevolent, and love doing a good action. Indeed, Sir, if I were alone in the world, I should scorn any remuneration, for virtue is its own reward; but a real moralist, your honour, must not forget his duties on any consideration, and I have a little family to whom my loss would be an irreparable injury; this, upon my honour, is my only inducement for taking advantage of your generosity;" and as the moralist ceased, he took out of his waistcoat pocket a paper, which he handed to me with his usual bow of deference.

I glanced over it—it was a bond, apparently drawn up in all the legal formalities, pledging myself, in case Job Jonson, before the expiration of three days, gave that information which should lead to the detection and punishment of the true murderers of Sir John Tyrrell, deceased, to ensure to the said Job Jonson the yearly annuity of three hundred pounds.

"It is with much pleasure that I shall sign this paper," said I; "but allow me (par parenthese) to observe, that since you only accept the annuity for the sake of benefiting your little family, in case of your death, this annuity, ceasing with your life, will leave your children as pennyless as at present."

"Pardon me, your honour," rejoined Job, not a whit daunted at the truth of my remark, "I can insure!"

"I forgot that," said I, signing, and restoring the paper; "and now to business."

Jonson gravely and carefully looked over the interesting document I returned to him, and carefully lapping it in three envelopes, inserted it in a huge red pocket-book, which he thrust into an innermost pocket in his waistcoat.

"Right, Sir," said he, slowly, "to business. Before I begin, you must, however, promise me, upon your honour as a gentleman, the strictest secrecy, as to my communications."

I readily agreed to this, so far as that secrecy did not impede my present object; and Job being content with this condition, resumed.

"You must forgive me, if, in order to arrive at the point in question, I set out from one which may seem to you a little distant."

I nodded my assent, and Job continued.

"I have known Dawson for some years; my acquaintance with him commenced at Newmarket, for I have always had a slight tendency to the turf. He was a wild, foolish fellow, easily led into any mischief, but ever the first to sneak out of it; in short, when he became one of us, which his extravagance soon compelled him to do, we considered him as a very serviceable tool, but one, that while he was quite wicked enough to begin a bad action, was much too weak to go through with it; accordingly he was often employed, but never trusted. By the word us, which I see has excited your curiosity, I merely mean a body corporate, established furtively, and restricted solely to exploits on the turf. I think it right to mention this, because I have the honour to belong to many other societies to which Dawson could never have been admitted. Well, Sir, our club was at last broken up, and Dawson was left to shift for himself. His father was still alive, and the young hopeful having quarrelled with him, was in the greatest distress. He came to me with a pitiful story, and a more pitiful face; so I took compassion upon the poor devil, and procured him, by dint of great interest, admission into a knot of good fellows, whom I visited, by the way, last night. Here I took him under my especial care; and as far as I could, with such a dull-headed dromedary, taught him some of the most elegant arts of my profession. However, the ungrateful dog soon stole back to his old courses, and robbed me of half my share of a booty to which I had helped him myself. I hate treachery and ingratitude, your honour; they are so terribly ungentlemanlike.

"I then lost sight of him, till between two and three months ago, when he returned to town, and attended our meetings with Tom Thornton, who had been chosen a member of the club some months before. Since we had met, Dawson's father had died, and I thought his flash appearance in town arose from his new inheritance. I was mistaken: old Dawson had tied up the property so tightly, that the young one could not scrape enough to pay his debts; accordingly, before he came to town, he gave up his life interest in the property to his creditors. However that be, Master Dawson seemed at the top of Fortune's wheel. He kept his horses, and sported the set to champagne and venison; in short, there would have been no end to his extravagance, had not Thornton sucked him like a leech.

"It was about that time, that I asked Dawson for a trifle to keep me from jail; for I was ill in bed, and could not help myself. Will you believe, Sir, that the rascal told me to go and be d—d, and Thornton said amen? I did not forget the ingratitude of my protege, though when I recovered I appeared entirely to do so. No sooner could I walk about, than I relieved all my necessities. He is but a fool who starves, with all London before him. In proportion as my finances increased, Dawson's visibly decayed. With them, decreased also his spirits. He became pensive and downcast; never joined any of our parties, and gradually grew quite a useless member of the corporation. To add to his melancholy, he was one morning present at the execution of an unfortunate associate of ours: this made a deep impression upon him; from that moment, he became thoroughly moody and despondent. He was frequently heard talking to himself, could not endure to be left alone in the dark, and began rapidly to pine away.

"One night, when he and I were seated together, he asked me if I never repented of my sins, and then added, with a groan, that I had never committed the heinous crime he had. I pressed him to confess, but he would not. However, I coupled that half avowal with his sudden riches and the mysterious circumstances of Sir John Tyrrell's death, and dark suspicions came into my mind. At that time, and indeed ever since Dawson re-appeared, we were often in the habit of discussing the notorious murder which then engrossed public attention; and as Dawson and Thornton had been witnesses on the inquest, we frequently referred to them respecting it. Dawson always turned pale, and avoided the subject; Thornton, on the contrary, brazened it out with his usual impudence. Dawson's aversion to the mention of the murder now came into my remembrance with double weight to strengthen my suspicions; and, on conversing with one or two of our comrades, I found that my doubts were more than shared, and that Dawson had frequently, when unusually oppressed with his hypochondria, hinted at his committal of some dreadful crime, and at his unceasing remorse for it.

"By degrees, Dawson grew worse and worse—his health decayed, he started at a shadow—drank deeply, and spoke, in his intoxication, words that made the hairs of our green men stand on end.

"We must not suffer this," said Thornton, whose hardy effrontery enabled him to lord it over the jolly boys, as if he were their dimber-damber; "his ravings and humdurgeon will unman all our youngsters." And so, under this pretence, Thornton had the unhappy man conveyed away to a secret asylum, known only to the chiefs of the gang, and appropriated to the reception of persons who, from the same weakness as Dawson, were likely to endanger others, or themselves. There many a poor wretch has been secretly immured, and never suffered to revisit the light of Heaven. The moon's minions, as well as the monarch's, must have their state prisoners, and their state victims.

"Well, Sir, I shall not detain you much longer. Last night, after your obliging confidence, I repaired to the meeting; Thornton was there, and very much out of humour. When our messmates dropped off, and we were alone, at one corner of the room, I began talking to him carelessly about his accusation of your friend, whom I have since learnt is Sir Reginald Glanville—an old friend of mine too; aye, you may look, Sir, but I can stake my life to having picked his pocket one night at the Opera. Thornton was greatly surprised at my early intelligence of a fact, hitherto kept so profound a secret; however, I explained it away by a boast of my skill in acquiring information: and he then incautiously let out, that he was exceedingly vexed with himself for the charge he had made against the prisoner, and very uneasy at the urgent inquiries set on foot for Dawson. More and more convinced of his guilt, I quitted the meeting, and went to Dawson's retreat.

"For fear of his escape, Thornton had had him closely confined to one of the most secret rooms in the house. His solitude and the darkness of the place, combined with his remorse, had worked upon a mind, never too strong, almost to insanity. He was writhing with the most acute and morbid pangs of conscience that my experience, which has been pretty ample, ever witnessed. The old hag, who is the Hecate (you see, Sir, I have had a classical education) of the place, was very loth to admit me to him, for Thornton had bullied her into a great fear of the consequences of disobeying his instructions; but she did not dare to resist my orders. Accordingly I had a long interview with the unfortunate man; he firmly believes that Thornton intends to murder him; and says, that if he could escape from his dungeon, he would surrender himself up to the first magistrate he could find.

"I told him that an innocent man had been apprehended for the crime of which I knew he and Thornton were guilty; and then taking upon myself the office of a preacher, I exhorted him to atone, as far as possible, for his past crime, by a full and faithful confession; that would deliver the innocent, and punish the guilty. I held out to him the hope that this confession might perhaps serve the purpose of king's evidence, and obtain him a pardon for his crime; and I promised to use my utmost zeal and diligence to promote his escape from his present den.

"He said, in answer, that he did not wish to live; that he suffered the greatest tortures of mind; and that the only comfort earth held out to him would be to ease his remorse by a full acknowledgment of his crime, and to hope for future mercy by expiating his offence on the scaffold; all this, and much more, to the same purpose, the hen-hearted fellow told me with sighs and groans. I would fain have taken his confession on the spot, and carried it away with me, but he refused to give it to me, or to any one but a parson, whose services he implored me to procure him. I told him, at first, that the thing was impossible; but, moved by his distress and remorse, I promised, at last, to bring one tonight, who should both administer spiritual comfort to him and receive his deposition. My idea at the moment was to disguise myself in the dress of the pater cove, [Note: A parson, or minister—but generally applied to a priest of the lowest order.] and perform the double job—since then I have thought of a better scheme.

"As my character, you see, your honour, is not so highly prized by the magistrates as it ought to be, any confession made to me might not be of the same value as if it were made to any one else— to a gentleman like you, for instance; and, moreover, it will not do for me to appear in evidence against any of the fraternity; and for two reasons: first, because I have taken a solemn oath never to do so; and, secondly, because I have a very fair chance of joining Sir John Tyrrell in kingdom come if I do. My present plan, therefore, if it meets your concurrence, would be to introduce your honour as the parson, and for you to receive the confession, which, indeed, you might take down in writing. This plan, I candidly confess, is not without great difficulty and some danger; for I have not only to impose you upon Dawson as a priest, but also upon Brimstone Bess as one of our jolly boys; for I need not tell you that any real parson might knock a long time at her door before it could be opened to him. You must, therefore, be as mum as a mole, unless she cants to you, and your answers must then be such as I shall dictate, otherwise she may detect you, and, should any of the true men be in the house, we should both come off worse than we went in."

"My dear Mr. Job," replied I, "there appears to me to be a much easier plan than all this; and that is, simply to tell the Bow-street officers where Dawson may be found, and I think they would be able to carry him away from the arms of Mrs. Brimstone Bess without any great difficulty or danger."

Jonson smiled.

"I should not long enjoy my annuity, your honour, if I were to set the runners upon our best hive. I should be stung to death before the week was out. Even you, should you accompany me to-night, will never know where the spot is situated, nor would you discover it again if you searched all London, with the whole police at your back. Besides, Dawson is not the only person in the house for whom the law is hunting—there are a score others whom I have no desire to give up to the gallows—hid among the odds and ends of the house, as snug as plums in a pudding. God forbid that I should betray them, and for nothing too! No, your honour, the only plan I can think of is the one I proposed; if you do not approve of it, and it certainly is open to exception, I must devise some other: but that may require delay."

"No, my good Job," replied I, "I am ready to attend you: but could we not manage to release Dawson, as well as take his deposition?—his personal evidence is worth all the written ones in the world."

"Very true," answered Job, "and if it be possible to give Bess the slip, we will. However, let us not lose what we may get by grasping at what we may not; let us have the confession first, and we'll try for the release afterwards. I have another reason for this, Sir, which, if you knew as much of penitent prigs as I do, you would easily understand. However, it may be explained by the old proverb, of 'the devil was sick,' As long as Dawson is stowed away in a dark hole, and fancies devils in every corner, he may be very anxious to make confessions, which, in broad day-light, might not seem to him so desirable. Darkness and solitude are strange stimulants to the conscience, and we may as well not lose any advantage they give us."

"You are an admirable reasoner," cried I, "and I am impatient to accompany you — at what hour shall it be?"

"Not much before midnight," answered Jonson, "but your honour must go back to school and learn lessons before then. Suppose Bess were to address you thus: 'Well you parish bull prig, are you for lushing jackey, or pattering in the hum box?' [Note: Well, you parson thief, are you for drinking gin, or talking in the pulpit?] I'll be bound you would not know how to answer."

"I am afraid you are right, Mr. Jonson," said I, in a tone of self-humiliation.

"Never mind," replied the compassionate Job, "we are all born ignorant— knowledge is not learnt in a day. A few of the most common and necessary words in our St. Giles's Greek, I shall be able to teach you before night; and I will, beforehand, prepare the old lady for seeing a young hand in the profession. As I must disguise you before we go, and that cannot well be done here, suppose you dine with me at my lodgings."

"I shall be too happy," said I, not a little surprised at the offer.

"I am in Charlotte-street, Bloomsbury, No. —. You must ask for me by the name of Captain Douglas," said Job, with dignity, "and we'll dine at five, in order to have time for your preliminary initiation."

"With all my heart," said I; and Mr. Job Jonson then rose, and reminding me of my promise of secrecy, took his departure.

CHAPTER LXXXI.

Pectus praeceptis format amicis.
—Horace.

Est quodam prodire tenus, si non datur ultra.
—Horace.

With all my love of enterprise and adventure, I cannot say that I should have particularly chosen the project before me for my evening's amusement, had I been left solely to my own will; but Glanville's situation forbade me to think of self, and so far from shrinking at the danger to which I was about to be exposed, I looked forward with the utmost impatience to the hour of rejoining Jonson.

There was yet a long time upon my hands before five o'clock; and the thought of Ellen left me in no doubt how it should be passed. I went to Berkeley-square; Lady Glanville rose eagerly when I entered the drawing- room.

"Have you seen Reginald?" said she, "or do you know where he has gone to?"

I answered, carelessly, that he had left town for a few days, and, I believed, merely upon a vague excursion, for the benefit of the country air.

"You reassure us," said Lady Glanville; "we have been quite alarmed by Seymour's manner. He appeared so confused when he told us Reginald left town, that I really thought some accident had happened to him."

I sate myself by Ellen, who appeared wholly occupied in the formation of a purse. While I was whispering into her ear words, which brought a thousand blushes to her cheek, Lady Glanville interrupted me, by an exclamation of "Have you seen the papers to-day, Mr. Pelham?" and on my reply in the negative, she pointed to an article in the Morning Herald, which she said had occupied their conjectures all the morning—it ran thus:—

"The evening before last, a person of rank and celebrity, was privately carried before the Magistrate at—. Since then, he has undergone an examination, the nature of which, as well as the name of the individual, is as yet kept a profound secret."

I believe that I have so firm a command over my countenance, that I should not change tint nor muscle, to hear of the greatest calamity that could happen to me. I did not therefore betray a single one of the emotions this paragraph excited within me, but appeared, on the contrary, as much at a loss as Lady Glanville, and wondered and guessed with her, till she remembered my present situation in the family, and left me alone with Ellen.

Why should the tete-a-tete of lovers be so uninteresting to the world— when there is scarcely a being in it who has not loved. The expressions of every other feeling comes home to us all—the expressions of love weary and fatigue us. But the interview of that morning, was far from resembling those which the maxims of love at that early period of its existence would assert. I could not give myself up to happiness which might so soon be disturbed, and though I veiled my anxiety and coldness from Ellen, I felt it as a crime to indulge even the appearance of transport, while Glanville lay alone, and in prison, with the charges of murder yet uncontroverted, and the chances of its doom undiminshed.

The clock had struck four before I left Ellen's, and without returning to my hotel, I threw myself into a hackney coach, and drove to Charlotte- street. The worthy Job received me with his wonted dignity and ease; his lodgings consisted of a first floor, furnished according to all the notions of Bloomsbury elegance—viz. new, glaring Brussels carpeting; convex mirrors, with massy gilt frames, and eagles at the summit; rosewood chairs, with chintz cushions; bright grates, with a flower-pot, cut out of yellow paper, in each; in short, all that especial neatness of upholstering paraphernalia, which Vincent used not inaptly, to designate by the title of "the tea-chest taste." Jonson seemed not a little proud of his apartments— accordingly, I complimented him upon their elegance.

"Under the rose be it spoken," said he, "the landlady, who is a widow, believes me to be an officer on half pay, and thinks I wish to marry her; poor woman, my black locks and green coat have a witchery that surprises even me: who would be a slovenly thief, when there are such advantages in being a smart one?"

"Right, Mr. Jonson!" said I; "but shall I own to you that I am surprised that a gentleman of your talents should stoop to the lower arts of the profession. I always imagined that pickpocketing was a part of your business left only to the plebeian purloiner; now I know, to my cost, that you do not disdain that manual accomplishment."

"Your honour speaks like a judge," answered Job: "the fact is, that I should despise what you rightly designate 'the lower arts of the profession,' if I did not value myself upon giving them a charm, and investing them with a dignity never bestowed upon them before. To give you an idea of the superior dexterity with which I manage my slight of hand, know, that four times I have been in that shop where you saw me borrow the diamond ring, which you now remark upon my little finger; and four times have I brought back some token of my visitations; nay, the shopman is so far from suspecting me, that he has twice favoured me with the piteous tale of the very losses I myself brought upon him; and I make no doubt that I shall hear in a few days, the whole history of the departed diamond, now in my keeping, coupled with your honour's appearance and custom. Allow that it would be a pity to suffer pride to stand in the way of the talents with which Providence has blest me; to scorn the little delicacies of art, which I execute so well, would, in my opinion, be as absurd as for an epic poet to disdain the composition of a perfect epigram, or a consummate musician, the melody of a faultless song."

"Bravo! Mr. Job," said I; "a truly great man, you see, can confer honour upon trifles." More I might have said, but was stopt short by the entrance of the landlady, who was a fine, fair, well dressed, comely woman, of about thirty-nine years and eleven months; or, to speak less precisely, between thirty and forty. She came to announce that dinner was served below. We descended, and found a sumptuous repast of roast beef and fish; this primary course was succeeded by that great dainty with common people—a duck and green peas.

"Upon my word, Mr. Jonson," said I, "you fare like a prince; your weekly expenditure must be pretty considerable for a single gentleman."

"I don't know," answered Jonson, with an air of lordly indifference—"I have never paid my good hostess any coin but compliments, and, in all probability, never shall."

Was there ever a better illustration of Moore's admonition—

'O, ladies, beware of a gay young knight,

After dinner, we remounted to the apartments Job emphatically called his own; and he then proceeded to initiate me in those phrases of the noble language of "Flash," which might best serve my necessities on the approaching occasion. The slang part of my Cambridge education had made me acquainted with some little elementary knowledge, which rendered Jonson's precepts less strange and abstruse. In this lecture, "sweet and holy," the hours passed away till it became time for me to dress. Mr. Jonson then took me into the penetralia of his bed-room. I stumbled against an enormous trunk. On hearing the involuntary anathema this accident conjured up to my lips, Jonson said—"Ah, Sir!—do oblige me by trying to move that box."

I did so, but could not stir it an inch.

"Your honour never saw a jewel box so heavy before, I think," said Jonson, with a smile.

"A jewel box!" I repeated.

"Yes," returned Jonson—"a jewel box, for it is full of precious stones! When I go away—not a little in my good landlady's books—I shall desire her, very importantly, to take the greatest care of 'my box.' Egad! it would be a treasure to MacAdam: he might pound its flinty contents into a street."

With these words, Mr. Jonson unlocked a wardrobe in the room, and produced a full suit of rusty black.

"There!" said he, with an air of satisfaction—"there! this will be your first step to the pulpit."

I doffed my own attire, and with "some natural sighs," at the deformity of my approaching metamorphosis, I slowly inducted myself in the clerical garments: they were much too wide, and a little too short for me; but Jonson turned me round, as if I were his eldest son, breeched for the first time—and declared, with an emphatical oath, that the clothes fitted me to a hair.

My host next opened a tin dressing box, of large dimensions, from which he took sundry powders, lotions, and paints. Nothing but my extreme friendship for Glanville could ever have supported me through the operation I then underwent. My poor complexion, thought I, with tears in my eyes, it is ruined for ever. To crown all—Jonson robbed me, by four clips of his scissars, of the luxuriant locks which, from the pampered indulgence so long accorded to them, might have rebelled against the new dynasty, which Jonson now elected to the crown. This consisted of a shaggy, but admirably made wig, of a sandy colour. When I was thus completely attired from head to foot, Job displayed me to myself before a full length looking glass.

Had I gazed at the reflection for ever, I should not have recognized either my form or visage. I thought my soul had undergone a real transmigration, and not carried to its new body a particle of the original one. What appeared the most singular was, that I did not seem even to myself at all a ridiculous or outre figure; so admirably had the skill of Mr. Jonson been employed. I overwhelmed him with encomiums, which he took au pied de la lettre. Never, indeed, was there a man so vain of being a rogue.

"But," said I, "why this disguise? Your friends will, probably, be well versed enough in the mysteries of metamorphosis, to see even through your arts; and, as they have never beheld me before, it would very little matter if I went in propria persona."

"True," answered Job, "but you don't reflect that without disguise you may hereafter be recognized; our friends walk in Bond-street, as well as your honour; and, in that case, you might be shot without a second, as the saying is."

"You have convinced me," said I; "and now, before we start, let me say one word further respecting our object. I tell you, fairly, that I think Dawson's written deposition but a secondary point; and, for this reason, should it not be supported by any circumstantial or local evidence, hereafter to be ascertained, it may be quite insufficient fully to acquit Glanville (in spite of all appearances), and criminate the real murderers. If, therefore, it be possible to carry off Dawson, after having secured his confession, we must. I think it right to insist more particularly on this point, as you appeared to me rather averse to it this morning."

"I say ditto to your honour," returned Job; "and you may be sure that I shall do all in my power to effect your object, not only from that love of virtue which is implanted in my mind, when no stronger inducement leads me astray, but from the more worldly reminiscence, that the annuity we have agreed upon is only to be given in case of success—not merely for well meaning attempts. To say that I have no objection to the release of Dawson, would be to deceive your honour; I own that I have; and the objection is, first, my fear lest he should peach respecting other affairs besides the murder of Sir John Tyrrell; and, secondly, my scruples as to appearing to interfere with his escape. Both of these chances expose me to great danger; however, one does not get three hundred a year for washing one's hands, and I must balance the one by the other."

"You are a sensible man, Mr. Job," said I; "and I am sure you will richly earn, and long enjoy your annuity."

As I said this, the watchman beneath our window, called "past eleven," and Jonson, starting up, hastily changed his own gay gear for a more simple dress, and throwing over all a Scotch plaid, gave me a similar one, in which I closely wrapped myself. We descended the stairs softly, and Jonson let us out into the street, by the "open sesame" of a key, which he retained about his person.

CHAPTER LXXXII.

Et cantare pares, et respondere parati.
                        —Virgil.

As we walked on into Tottenham-court-road, where we expected to find a hackney coach, my companion earnestly and strenuously impressed on my mind, the necessity of implicitly obeying any instructions or hints he might give me in the course of our adventure. "Remember," said he, forcibly, "that the least deviation from them, will not only defeat our object of removing Dawson, but even expose our lives to the most imminent peril." I faithfully promised to conform to the minutest tittle of his instructions.

We came to a stand of coaches. Jonson selected one, and gave the coachman an order; he took care it should not reach my ears. During the half hour we passed in this vehicle, Job examined and reexamined me in my "canting catechism," as he termed it. He expressed himself much pleased with the quickness of my parts, and honoured me with an assurance that in less than three months he would engage to make me as complete a ruffler as ever nailed a swell.

To this gratifying compliment I made the best return in my power.

"You must not suppose," said Jonson—some minutes afterwards, "from our use of this language, that our club consists of the lower order of thieves—quite the contrary: we are a knot of gentlemen adventurers who wear the best clothes, ride the best hacks, frequent the best gaming houses, as well as the genteelest haunts, and sometimes keep the first company in London. We are limited in number: we have nothing in common with ordinary prigs, and should my own little private amusements (as you appropriately term them) be known in the set, I should have a very fair chance of being expelled for ungentlemanlike practices. We rarely condescend to speak "flash" to each other in our ordinary meetings, but we find it necessary, for many shifts to which fortune sometimes drives us. The house you are going this night to visit, is a sort of colony we have established for whatever persons amongst us are in danger of blood- money. [Rewards for the apprehension of thieves.] There they sometimes lie concealed for weeks together, and are at last shipped off for the continent, or enter the world under a new alias. To this refuge of the distressed we also send any of the mess, who, like Dawson, are troubled with qualms of conscience, which are likely to endanger the commonwealth; there they remain, as in a hospital, till death, or a cure, in short, we put the house, like its inmates, to any purposes likely to frustrate our enemies, and serve ourselves. Old Brimstone Bess, to whom I shall introduce you, is, as I before said, the guardian of the place; and the language that re- spectable lady chiefly indulges in, is the one into which you have just acquired so good an insight. Partly in compliment to her, and partly from inclination, the dialect adopted in her house, is almost entirely "flash;" and you, therefore, perceive the necessity of appear- ing not utterly ignorant of a tongue, which is not only the language of the country, but one with which no true boy, however high in his profession, is ever unacquainted."

By the time Jonson had finished this speech, the coach stopped—I looked eagerly out—Jonson observed the motion: "We have not got half-way yet, your honour," said he. We left the coach, which Jonson requested me to pay, and walked on.

"Tell me frankly, Sir," said Job, "do you know where you are?"

"Not in the least," replied I, looking wistfully up a long, dull, ill-lighted street.

Job rolled his sinister eye towards me with a searching look, and then turning abruptly to the right, penetrated into a sort of covered lane, or court, which terminated in an alley, that brought us sud- denly to a stand of three coaches; one of these Job hailed—we en- tered it—a secret direction was given, and we drove furiously on, faster than I should think the crazy body of hackney chariot ever drove before. I observed, that we had now entered a part of the town, which was singularly strange to me; the houses were old, and for the most part of the meanest description; we appeared to me to be threading a labyrinth of alleys; once, I imagined that I caught, through a sudden opening, a glimpse of the river, but we passed so rapidly, that my eye might have deceived me. At length we stopped: the coachman was again dismissed, and I again walked onwards, under the guidance, and almost at the mercy of my honest companion.

Jonson did not address me—he was silent and absorbed, and I had therefore full leisure to consider my present situation. Though (thanks to my physical constitution) I am as callous to fear as most men, a few chilling apprehensions, certainly flitted across my mind, when I looked round at the dim and dreary sheds—houses they were not—which were on either side of our path; only here and there, a single lamp shed a sickly light upon the dismal and inter- secting lanes (though lane is too lofty a word), through which our footsteps woke a solitary sound. Sometimes this feeble light was altogether withheld, and I could scarcely catch even the outline of my companion's muscular frame. However, he strode on through the darkness, with the mechanical rapidity of one to whom every stone is familiar. I listened eagerly for the sound of the watchman's voice, in vain—that note was never heard in those desolate recesses. My ear drank in nothing but the sound of our own footsteps, or the occasional burst of obscene and unholy merriment from some half- closed hovel, where infamy and vice were holding revels. Now and then, a wretched thing, in the vilest extreme of want, and loath- someness, and rags, loitered by the unfrequent lamps, and inter- rupted our progress with solicitations, which made my blood run cold. By degrees even these tokens of life ceased—the last lamp was entirely shut from our view—we were in utter darkness.

"We are near our journey's end now," whispered Jonson

At these words a thousand unwelcome reflections forced them- selves voluntarily on my mind: I was about to plunge into the most secret retreat of men whose long habits of villany and desperate abandonment, had hardened into a nature which had scarcely a sympathy with my own; unarmed and defenceless, I was going to penetrate a concealment upon which their lives perhaps depended; what could I anticipate from their vengeance, but the sure hand and the deadly knife, which their self- preservation would more than justify to such lawless reasoners. And who was my companion? One, who literally gloried in the perfection of his nefarious practices; and who, if he had stopped short of the worst enormities, seemed neither to disown the principle upon which they were committed, nor to balance for a moment between his interest and his conscience.

Nor did he attempt to conceal from me the danger to which I was exposed; much as his daring habits of life, and the good fortune which had attended him, must have hardened his nerves, even he, seemed fully sensible of the peril he incurred — a peril certainly considerably less than that which attended my temerity. Bitterly did I repent, as these reflections rapidly passed my mind, my negligence in not providing myself with a single weapon in case of need: the worst pang of death, is the falling without a struggle.

However, it was no moment for the indulgence of fear, it was rather one of those eventful periods which so rarely occur in the monotony of common life, when our minds are sounded to their utmost depths: and energies of which we dreamt not, when at rest in their secret retreats, arise like spirits at the summons of the wizard, and bring to the invoking mind, an unlooked for and preternatural aid.

There was something too in the disposition of my guide, which gave me a confidence in him, not warranted by the occupations of his life; an easy and frank boldness, an ingenuous vanity of abilities, skilfully, though dishonestly exerted, which had nothing of the meanness and mystery of an ordinary villain, and which being equally prominent with the rascality they adorned, prevented the attention from dwelling only upon the darker shades of his character. Besides, I had so closely entwined his interest with my own, that I felt there could be no possible ground either for suspecting him of any deceit towards me, or of omitting any art or exertion which could conduce to our mutual safety or our common end.

Forcing myself to dwell solely upon the more encouraging side of the enterprise I had undertaken, we continued to move on, silent and in darkness, for some minutes longer — Jonson then halted.

"Are you quite prepared, Sir?" said he, in a whisper: "if your heart fails, in God's name let us turn back: the least evident terror will be as much as your life is worth."

My thoughts were upon Sir Reginald and Ellen, as I replied—

"You have told and convinced me that I may trust is you, and I have no fears; my present object is one as strong to me as life."

"I would we had a glim," rejoined Job, musingly; "I should like to see your face: but will you give me your hand, Sir?"

I did, and Jonson held it in his own for more than a minute.

"'Fore Heaven, Sir," said he, at last, "I would you were one of us. You would live a brave man and die a game one. Your pulse is like iron; and your hand does not sway—no—not so much as to wave a dove's feather; it would be a burning shame if harm came to so stout a heart." Job moved on a few steps. "Now, Sir," he whispered, "remember your flash; do exactly as I may have occasion to tell you; and be sure to sit away from the light, should we be in company."

With these words he stopped. I perceived by the touch, for it was too dark to see, that he was leaning down, apparently in a listening attitude; presently, he tapped five times at what I supposed was a door, though I afterwards discovered it was the shutter to a window; upon this, a faint light broke through the crevices of the boards, and a low voice uttered some sound, which my ear did not catch. Job replied, in the same key, and in words which were perfectly unintelligible to me; the light disappeared; Job moved round, as if turning a corner. I heard the heavy bolts and bars of a door slowly withdraw; and in a few moments, a harsh voice said, in the thieves' dialect,

"Ruffling Job, my prince of prigs, is that you? are you come to the ken alone, or do you carry double?"

"Ah, Bess, my covess, strike me blind if my sees don't tout your bingo muns in spite of the darkmans. Egad, you carry a bane blink aloft. Come to the ken alone—no! my blowen; did not I tell you I should bring a pater cove, to chop up the whiners for Dawson?"

"Stubble it, you ben, you deserve to cly the jerk for your patter; come in, and be d—d to you."

Upon this invitation, Jonson, seizing me by the arm, pushed me into the house, and followed. "Go for a glim, Bess, to light in the parish bull with proper respect. I'll close the gig of the crib."

At this order, delivered in an authoritative tone, the old woman, mumbling "strange oaths" to herself, moved away; when she was out of hearing, Job whispered,

"Mark, I shall leave the bolts undrawn, the door opens with a latch, which you press thus—do not forget the spring; it is easy, but peculiar; should you be forced to run for it, you will also remember, above all, when you are out of the door, to turn to the right and go straight forwards."

The old woman now reappeared with a light, and Jonson ceased, and moved hastily towards her: I followed. The old woman asked whether the door had been carefully closed, and Jonson, with an oath at her doubts of such a matter, answered in the affirmative.

We proceeded onwards, through a long and very narrow passage, till Bess opened a small door to the left, and introduced us into a large room, which, to my great dismay, I found already occupied by four men, who were sitting, half immersed in smoke, by an oak table, with a capacious bowl of hot liquor before them. At the back ground of this room, which resembled the kitchen of a public house, was an enormous skreen, of antique fashion; a low fire burnt sullenly in the grate, and beside it was one of those high-backed chairs, seem frequently in old houses, and old pictures. A clock stood in one corner, and in the opposite nook were a flight of narrow stairs, which led downwards, probably to a cellar. On a row of shelves, were various bottles of the different liquors generally in request among the "flash" gentry, together with an old-fashioned fiddle, two bridles, and some strange looking tools, probably of more use to true boys than honest men.

Brimstone Bess was a woman about the middle size, but with bones and sinews which would not have disgraced a prize-fighter; a cap, that might have been cleaner, was rather thrown than put on the back of her head, developing, to full advantage, the few scanty locks of grizzled ebon which adorned her countenance. Her eyes large, black, and prominent, sparkled with a fire half vivacious, half vixen. The nasal feature was broad and fungous, and, as well as the whole of her capacious physiognomy, blushed with the deepest scarlet: it was evident to see that many a full bottle of "British compounds" had contributed to the feeding of that burning and phosphoric illumination, which was, indeed, "the outward and visible sign of an inward and spiritual grace."

The expression of the countenance was not wholly bad. Amidst the deep traces of searing vice and unrestrained passion; amidst all that was bold, and unfeminine, and fierce, and crafty, there was a latent look of coarse good humour, a twinkle of the eye that bespoke a tendency to mirth and drollery, and an upward curve of the lip that shewed, however the human creature might be debased, it still cherished its grand characteristic — the propensity to laughter.

The garb of this dame Leonarda was by no means of that humble nature which one might have supposed. A gown of crimson silk, flounced and furbelowed to the knees, was tastefully relieved by a bright yellow shawl; and a pair of heavy pendants glittered in her ears, which were of the size proper to receive "the big words" they were in the habit of hearing. Probably this finery had its origin in the policy of her guests, who had seen enough of life to know that age, which tames all other passions, never tames the passion of dress in a woman's mind.

No sooner did the four revellers set their eyes upon me than they all rose.

"Zounds, Bess!" cried the tallest of them, "what cull's this? Is this a bowsing ken for every cove to shove his trunk in?"

"What ho, my kiddy," cried Job, "don't be glimflashy: why you'd cry beef on a blater; the cove is a bob cull, and a pal of my own; and, moreover, is as pretty a Tyburn blossom as ever was brought up to ride a horse foaled by an acorn."

Upon this commendatory introduction I was forthwith surrounded, and one of the four proposed that I should be immediately "elected."

This motion, which was probably no gratifying ceremony, Job negatived with a dictatorial air, and reminded his comrades that however they might find it convenient to lower themselves occasionally, yet that they were gentlemen sharpers, and not vulgar cracksmen and cly-fakers, and that, therefore, they ought to welcome me with the good breeding appropriate to their station.

Upon this hint, which was received with mingled laughter and deference, for Job seemed to be a man of might among these Philistines, the tallest of the set, who bore the euphonious appellation of Spider-shanks, politely asked me if I would "blow a cloud with him?" and, upon my assent—for I thought such an occupation would be the best excuse for silence—he presented me with a pipe of tobacco, to which dame Brimstone applied a light, and I soon lent my best endeavours to darken still further the atmosphere around us.

Mr. Job Jonson then began artfully to turn the conversation away from me to the elder confederates of his crew; these were all spoken of under certain singular appellations which might well baffle impertinent curiosity. The name of one was "the Gimblet," another "Crack Crib," a third, the "Magician," a fourth, "Cherry coloured Jowl." The tallest of the present company was called (as I before said) "Spider-shanks," and the shortest "Fib Fakescrew;" Job himself was honoured by the venerabile nomen of "Guinea Pig." At last Job explained the cause of my appearance; viz. his wish to pacify Dawson's conscience by dressing up one of the pals, whom the sinner could not recognize, as an "autem bawler," and so obtaining him the benefit of the clergy without endangering the gang by his confession. This detail was received with great good humour, and Job, watching his opportunity, soon after rose, and, turning to me, said,

"Toddle, my bob cull. We must track up the dancers and tout the sinner."

I wanted no other hint to leave my present situation.

"The ruffian cly thee, Guinea Pig, for stashing the lush," said Spider- shanks, helping himself out of the bowl, which was nearly empty.

"Stash the lush!" cried Mrs. Brimstone, "aye, and toddle off to Ruggins. Why, you would not be boosing till lightman's in a square crib like mine, as if you were in a flash panny."

"That's bang up, mort!" cried Fib. "A square crib, indeed! aye, square as Mr. Newman's courtyard—ding boys on three sides, and the crap on the fourth!"

This characteristic witticism was received with great applause;
and Jonson, taking a candlestick from the fair fingers of the exas-
perated Mrs. Brimstone, the hand thus conveniently released, immediately transferred itself to Fib's cheeks, with so hearty a concus-
sion, that it almost brought the rash jester to the ground. Jonson and
I lost not a moment in taking advantage of the confusion this gentle
remonstrance appeared to occasion; but instantly left the room and
closed the door.

CHAPTER LXXXIII.

'Tis true that we are in great danger;
The greater, therefore, should our courage be.
—Shakspeare.

We proceeded a short way, when we were stopped by a door; this Job opened, and a narrow staircase, lighted from above, by a dim lamp, was before us. We ascended, and found ourselves in a sort of gallery; here hung another lamp, beneath which Job opened a closet.

"This is the place where Bess generally leaves the keys," said he, "we shall find them here, I hope."

So saying, Master Job entered, leaving me in the passage, but soon returned with a disappointed air.

"The old harridan has left them below," said he, "I must go down for them; your honour will wait here till I return."

Suiting the action to the word, honest Job immediately descended, leaving me alone with my own reflections. Just opposite to the closet was the door of some apartment; I leant accidentally against it; it was only a- jar, and gave way; the ordinary consequence in such accidents, is a certain precipitation from the centre of gravity. I am not exempt from the general lot; and accordingly entered the room in a manner entirely contrary to that which my natural incli-nation would have prompted me to adopt. My ear was accosted by a faint voice, which proceeded from a bed at the opposite corner; it asked, in the thieves' dialect, and in the feeble accents of bodily weakness, who was there? I did not judge it necessary to make any reply, but was withdrawing as gently as possible, when my eye rested upon a table at the foot of the bed, upon which, among two or three miscellaneous articles, were deposited a brace of pistols, and one of those admirable swords, made according to the modern military regulation, for the united purpose of cut and thrust. The light which enabled me to discover the contents of the room, proceeded from a rush- light placed in the grate; this general symptom of a valetudinarian, together with some other little odd matters (combined with the weak voice of the speaker), impressed me with the idea of having intruded into the chamber of some sick member of the crew. Emboldened by this notion, and by perceiving that the curtains were drawn closely around the bed, so that the inmate could have optical discernment of nothing that occurred without, I could not resist taking two soft steps to the table, and quietly removing a weapon whose bright face seemed to invite me as a long known and long tried friend.

This was not, however, done in so noiseless a manner, but what the voice again addressed me, in a somewhat louder key, by the appellation of "Brimstone Bess," asking, with sundry oaths, "What was the matter?" and requesting something to drink. I need scarcely say that, as before, I made no reply, but crept out of the room as gently as possible, blessing my good fortune for having thrown into my way a weapon with the use of which, above all others, I was best acquainted. Scarcely had I regained the passage, before Jonson re-appeared with the keys; I showed him my treasure (for indeed it was of no size to conceal).

"Are you mad, Sir?" said he, "or do you think that the best way to avoid suspicion, is to walk about with a drawn sword in your hand? I would not have Bess see you for the best diamond I ever borrowed." With these words Job took the sword from my reluctant hand.

"Where did you get it?" said he.

I explained in a whisper, and Job, re-opening the door I had so unceremoniously entered, laid the weapon softly on a chair that stood within reach. The sick man, whose senses were of course rendered doubly acute by illness, once more demanded in a fretful tone, who was there? And Job replied, in the flash language, that Bess had sent him up to look for her keys, which she imagined she had left there. The invalid rejoined, by a request to Jonson to reach him a draught, and we had to undergo a farther delay, until his petition was complied with; we then proceeded up the passage, till we came to another flight of steps, which led to a door: Job opened it, and we entered a room of no common dimensions.

"This," said he, "is Bess Brimstone's sleeping apartment; whoever goes into the passage that leads not only to Dawson's room, but to the several other chambers occupied by such of the gang as require particular care, must pass first through this room. You see that bell by the bedside—I assure you it is no ordinary tintannabulum; it communicates with every sleeping apartment in the house, and is only rung in cases of great alarm, when every boy must look well to himself; there are two more of this description, one in the room which we have just left, another in the one occupied by Spider-shanks, who is our watch-dog, and keeps his kennel below. Those steps in the common room, which seem to lead to a cellar, conduct to his den. As we shall have to come back through this room, you see the difficulty of smuggling Dawson—and if the old dame rung the alarm, the whole hive would be out in a moment."

After this speech, Job left the room, by opening a door at the opposite end, which shewed us a passage, similar in extent and fashion, to the one we had left below; at the very extremity of this was the entrance to an apartment at which Jonson stopped.

"Here," said he, taking from his pocket a small paper book, and an ink- horn; "here, your honour, take these, you may want to note the heads of Dawson's confession, we are now at his door." Job then applied one of the keys of a tolerably sized bunch to the door, and the next moment we were in Dawson's apartment.

The room which, though low and narrow, was of considerable length, was in utter darkness, and the dim and flickering light Jonson held, only struggled with, rather than penetrated the thick gloom. About the centre of the room stood the bed, and sitting upright on it, with a wan and hollow countenance, bent eagerly towards us, was a meagre, attenuated figure. My recollection of Dawson, whom, it will be remembered, I had only seen once before, was extremely faint, but it had impressed me with the idea of a middle sized and rather athletic man, with a fair and florid complexion: the creature I now saw, was totally the reverse of this idea. His cheeks were yellow and drawn in; his hand which was raised, in the act of holding aside the curtains, was like the talons of a famished vulture, so thin, so long, so withered in its hue and texture.

No sooner did the advancing light allow him to see us distinctly, than he half sprung from the bed, and cried, in that peculiar tone of joy, which seems to throw off from the breast a suffocating weight of previous terror and suspense, "Thank God, thank God! it is you at last; and you have brought the clergyman—God bless you, Jonson, you are a true friend to me."

"Cheer up, Dawson," said Job; "I have smuggled in this worthy gentleman, who, I have no doubt, will be of great comfort to you—but you must be open with him, and tell all."

"That I will—that I will," cried Dawson, with a wild and vindictive expression of countenance—"if it be only to hang him. Here, Jonson, give me your hand, bring the light nearer—I say—he, the devil—the fiend— has been here to-day, and threatened to murder me; and I have listened, and listened, all night, and thought I heard his step along the passage, and up the stairs, and at the door; but it was nothing, Job, nothing—and you are come at last, good, kind, worthy Job. Oh! 'tis so horrible to be left in the dark, and not sleep—and in this large, large room, which looks like eternity at night—and one does fancy such sights, Job—such horrid, horrid sights. Feel my wristband, Jonson, and here at my back, you would think they had been pouring water over me, but its only the cold sweat. Oh! it is a fearful thing to have a bad conscience, Job; but you won't leave me till daylight, now, that's a dear, good Job!"

"For shame, Dawson," said Jonson; "pluck up, and be a man; you are like a baby frightened by its nurse. Here's the clergyman come to heal your poor wounded conscience, will you hear him now?"

"Yes," said Dawson; "yes!—but go out of the room—I can't tell all if you're here; go, Job, go!—but you're not angry with me—I don't mean to offend you."

"Angry!" said Job; "Lord help the poor fellow! no, to be sure not. I'll stay outside the door till you've done with the clergyman—but make haste, for the night's almost over, and it's as much as the parson's life is worth to stay here after daybreak."

"I will make haste," said the guilty man, tremulously; "but, Job, where are you going—what are you doing? leave the light!—here, Job, by the bed-side."

Job did as he was desired, and quitted the room, leaving the door not so firmly shut, but that he might hear, if the penitent spoke aloud, every particular of his confession.

I seated myself on the side of the bed, and taking the skeleton hand of the unhappy man, spoke to him in the most consolatory and comforting words I could summon to my assistance. He seemed greatly soothed by my efforts, and at last implored me to let him join me in prayer. I knelt down, and my lips readily found words for that language, which, whatever be the formula of our faith, seems, in all emotions which come home to our hearts, the most natural method of expressing them. It is here, by the bed of sickness, or remorse, that the ministers of God have their real power! it is here, that their office is indeed a divine and unearthly mission; and that in breathing balm and comfort, in healing the broken heart, in raising the crushed and degraded spirit—they are the voice, and oracle of the FATHER, who made us in benevolence, and will judge of us in mercy! I rose, and after a short pause, Dawson, who expressed himself impatient of the comfort of confession, thus began—

"I have no time, Sir, to speak of the earlier part of my life. I passed it upon the race-course, and at the gaming-table—all that was, I know, very wrong, and wicked; but I was a wild, idle boy, and eager for any thing like enterprise or mischief. Well, Sir, it is now more than three years ago since I first met one Tom Thornton; it was at a boxing match. Tom was chosen chairman, at a sort of club of the farmers and yeomen; and being a lively, amusing fellow, and accustomed to the company of gentlemen, was a great favourite with all of us. He was very civil to me, and I was quite pleased with his notice. I did not, however, see much of him then, nor for more than two years afterwards; but some months ago we met again. I was in very poor circumstances, so was he, and this made us closer friends than we might otherwise have been. He lived a great deal at the gambling-houses, and fancied he had discovered a certain method of winning [Note: A very common delusion, both among sharpers and their prey.] at hazard. So, whenever he could not find a gentleman whom he could cheat with false dice, tricks at cards, he would go into any hell to try his infallible game. I did not, however, perceive, that he made a good livelihood by it; and though sometimes, either by that method or some other, he had large sums of money in his possession, yet they were spent as soon as acquired. The fact was, that he was not a man who could ever grow rich; he was extremely extravagant in all things—loved women and drinking, and was always striving to get into the society of people above him. In order to do this, he affected great carelessness of money; and if, at a race or a cock-fight, any real gentlemen would go home with him, he would insist upon treating them to the very best of every thing.

"Thus, Sir, he was always poor, and at his wit's end, for means to supply his extravagance. He introduced me to three or four gentlemen, as he called them, but whom I have since found to be markers, sharpers, and black-legs; and this set soon dissipated the little honesty my own habits of life had left me. They never spoke of things by their right names; and, therefore, those things never seemed so bad as they really were—to swindle a gentleman, did not sound a crime, when it was called 'macing a swell'—nor transportation a punishment, when it was termed, with a laugh, 'lagging a cove.' Thus, insensibly, my ideas of right and wrong, always obscure, became perfectly confused: and the habit of treating all crimes as subjects of jest in familiar conversation, soon made me regard them as matters of very trifling importance.

"Well, Sir, at Newmarket races, this Spring meeting, Thornton and I were on the look out. He had come down to stay, during the races, at a house I had just inherited from my father, but which was rather an expense to me than an advantage; especially as my wife, who was an innkeeper's daughter, was very careless and extravagant. It so happened that we were both taken in by a jockey, whom we had bribed very largely, and were losers to a very considerable amount. Among other people, I lost to a Sir John Tyrrell. I expressed my vexation to Thornton, who told me not to mind it, but to tell Sir John that I would pay him if he came to the town; and that he was quite sure we could win enough, by his certain game at hazard, to pay off my debt. He was so very urgent, that I allowed myself to be persuaded; though Thornton has since told me, that his only motive was, to prevent Sir John's going to the Marquess of Chester's (where he was invited) with my lord's party; and so, to have an opportunity of accomplishing the crime he then meditated.

"Accordingly, as Thornton desired, I asked Sir John Tyrrell to come with me to Newmarket. He did so. I left him, joined Thornton, and went to the gambling-house. Here we were engaged in Thornton's sure game, when Sir John entered. I went up and apologized for not paying, and said I would pay him in three months. However, Sir John was very angry, and treated me with such rudeness, that the whole table remarked it. When he was gone, I told Thornton how hurt and indignant I was at Sir John's treatment. He incensed me still more—exaggerated Sir John's conduct—said that I had suffered the grossest insult, and, at last, put me into such a passion, that I said, that if I was a gentleman, I would fight Sir John Tyrrell across a table.

"When Thornton saw I was so moved, he took me out of the room, and carried me to an inn. Here he ordered dinner, and several bottles of wine. I never could bear much drink: he knew this, and artfully plied me with wine till I scarcely knew what I did or said. He then talked much of our destitute situation—affected to put himself out of the question— said he was a single man, and could easily make shift upon a potatoe—but that I was encumbered with a wife and child, whom I could not suffer to starve. He then said, that Sir John Tyrrell had publicly disgraced me— that I should be blown upon the course—that no gentleman would bet with me again, and a great deal more of the same sort. Seeing what an effect he had produced upon me, he then told me that he had seen Sir John receive a large sum of money, that would more than pay our debts, and set us up like gentlemen: and, at last, he proposed to me to rob him. Intoxicated as I was, I was somewhat startled at this proposition. However, the slang terms in which Thornton disguised the greatness and danger of the offence, very much diminished both in my eyes—so at length I consented.

"We went to Sir John's inn, and learnt that he had just set out; accordingly, we mounted our horses, and rode after him. The night had already closed in. After we had got some distance from the main road, into a lane, which led both to my house and to Chester Park—for the former was on the direct way to my lord's—we passed a man on horseback. I only observed that he was wrapped in a cloak—but Thornton said, directly we had passed him, "I know that man well—he has been following Tyrrell all day—and though he attempts to screen himself, I have penetrated his disguise; he is Tyrrell's mortal enemy."

"'Should the worst come to the worst," added Thornton, (words which I did not at that moment understand) we can make him bear the blame.'"

"When we had got some way further, we came up to Tyrrell and a gentleman, whom, to our great dismay, we found that Sir John had joined—the gentleman's horse had met with an accident, and Thornton dismounted to offer his assistance. He assured the gentleman, who proved afterwards to be a Mr. Pelham, that the horse was quite lame, and that he would scarcely be able to get it home; and he then proposed to Sir John to accompany us, and said that we would put him in the right road; this offer Sir John rejected very haughtily, and we rode on.

"'It's all up with us,' said I; 'since he has joined another person.'

"'Not at all,' replied Thornton; 'for I managed to give the horse a sly poke with my knife; and if I know any thing of Sir John Tyrrell, he is much too impatient a spark to crawl along, a snail's pace, with any companion, especially with this heavy shower coming on.'

"'But,' said I, for I now began to recover from my intoxication, and to be sensible of the nature of our undertaking, 'the moon is up, and unless this shower conceals it, Sir John will recognize us; so you see, even if he leaves the gentleman, it will be no use, and we had much better make haste home and go to bed.'

"Upon this, Thornton cursed me for a faint-hearted fellow, and said that the cloud would effectually hide the moon—or, if not—he added—'I know how to silence a prating tongue.' At these words I was greatly alarmed, and said, that if he meditated murder as well as robbery, I would have nothing further to do with it. Thornton laughed, and told me not to be a fool. While we were thus debating, a heavy shower came on; we rode hastily to a large tree, by the side of a pond—which, though bare and withered, was the nearest shelter the country afforded, and was only a very short distance from my house. I wished to go home—but Thornton would not let me, and as I was always in the habit of yielding, I stood with him, though very reluctantly, under the tree.

"Presently, we heard the trampling of a horse.

"'It is he—it is he,' cried Thornton, with a savage tone of exulta-
tion— 'and alone!—Be ready—we must make a rush—I will be the
one to bid him to deliver—you hold your tongue.

"The clouds and rain had so overcast the night, that, although it
was not perfectly dark, it was sufficiently obscure to screen our
countenances. Just as Tyrrell approached, Thornton dashed forward, and cried, in a feigned voice—'Stand, on your peril!' I followed, and we were now both by Sir John's side.

"He attempted to push by us—but Thornton seized him by the
arm—there was a stout struggle, in which, as yet, I had no share—at
last, Tyrrell got loose from Thornton, and I seized him—he set spurs
to his horse, which was a very spirited and strong animal—it reared
upwards, and very nearly brought me and my horse to the
ground—at that instant, Thornton struck the unfortunate man a
violent blow across the head with the butt end of his heavy whip—
Sir John's hat had fallen before in the struggle, and the blow was so
stunning that it felled him upon the spot. Thornton dismounted,
and made me do the same—'There is no time to lose,' said he; 'let us
drag him from the roadside and rifle him.' We accordingly carried
him (he was still senseless) to the side of the pond before men-
tioned— while we were searching for the money Thornton spoke of,
the storm ceased, and the moon broke out—we were detained some
moments by the accident of Tyrrell's having transferred his pocket-
book from the pocket Thornton had seen him put it in on the race
ground to an inner one.

"We had just discovered, and seized the pocket-book, when Sir
John awoke from his swoon, and his eyes opened upon Thornton,
who was still bending over him, and looking at the contents of the
book to see that all was right; the moonlight left Tyrrell in no doubt
as to our persons; and struggling hard to get up, he cried, 'I know
you! I know you! you shall hang for this.' No sooner had he uttered
this imprudence, than it was all over with him. 'We will see that, Sir
John,' said Thornton, setting his knee upon Tyrrell's chest, and nail-
ing him down. While thus employed, he told me to feel in his coat-
pocket for a case-knife.

"'For God's sake!' cried Tyrrell, with a tone of agonizing terror which haunts me still, 'spare my life!'

"'It is too late,' said Thornton, deliberately, and taking the knife from my hands, he plunged it into Sir John's side, and as the blade was too short to reach the vitals, Thornton drew it backwards and forwards to widen the wound. Tyrrell was a strong man, and still continued to struggle and call out for mercy—Thornton drew out the knife—Tyrrell seized it by the blade, and his fingers were cut through before Thornton could snatch it from his grasp; the wretched gentleman then saw all hope was over; he uttered one loud, sharp, cry of despair. Thornton put one hand to his mouth, and with the other gashed his throat from ear to ear.

"'You have done for him, and for us now,' said I, as Thornton slowly rose from the body. 'No,' replied he, 'look, he still moves;' and sure enough he did, but it was in the last agony. However, Thornton, to make all sure, plunged the knife again into his body; the blade came into contact with a bone, and snapped in two; so great was the violence of the blow, that instead of remaining in the flesh, the broken piece fell upon the ground among the long fern and grass.

"While we were employed in searching for it: Thornton, whose ears were much sharper than mine, caught the sound of a horse. 'Mount! mount,' he cried; 'and let us be off.' We sprung up on our horses, and rode away as fast as we could. I wished to go home, as it was so near at hand; but Thornton insisted on making to an old shed, about a quarter of a mile across the fields; thither, therefore, we went."

"Stop," said I, "what did Thornton do with the remaining part of the case-knife? did he throw it away, or carry it with him?"

"He took it with him," answered Dawson, "for his name was engraved on a silver plate, on the handle; and, he was therefore afraid of throwing it into the pond, as I advised, lest at any time it should be discovered. Close by the shed, there is a plantation of young firs of some extent. Thornton and I entered, and he dug a hole with the broken blade of the knife, and buried it, covering up the hole again with the earth."

"Describe the place," said I. Dawson paused, and seemed to recollect; I was on the very tenterhooks of suspence, for I saw with one glance all the importance of his reply.

After some moments, he shook his head; "I cannot describe the place," said he, "for the wood is so thick: yet I know the exact spot so well, that were I in any part of the plantation, I could point it out immediately."

I told him to pause again, and recollect himself; and, at all events, to try to indicate the place. However, his account was so confused and perplexed, that I was forced to give up the point in despair, and he continued.

"After we had done this, Thornton told me to hold the horses, and said he would go alone, to spy whether we might return; accordingly he did so, and brought back word, in about half an hour, that he had crept cautiously along till in sight of the place, and then throwing himself down on his face by the ridge of a bank, had observed a man, (whom he was sure was the person with a cloak we had passed, and whom, he said, was Sir Reginald Glanville,) mount his horse on the very spot of the murder, and ride off, while another person (Mr. Pelham), appeared, and also discovered the fatal place.

"'There is no doubt now,' said he, 'that we shall have the hue-and cry upon us. However, if you are staunch and stout-hearted, no possible danger can come to us; for you may leave me alone to throw the whole guilt upon Sir Reginald Glanville.'

"'We then mounted, and rode home. We stole up stairs by the back-way— Thornton's linen and hands were stained with blood. The former he took off, locked up carefully, and burnt the first opportunity; the latter he washed; and that the water might not lead to detection, drank it. We then appeared as if nothing had occurred, and learnt that Mr. Pelham had been to the house; but as, very fortunately, our out-buildings had been lately robbed by some idle people, the wife and servants had refused to admit him. I was thrown into great agitation, and was extremely frightened. However, as Mr. Pelham had left a message that we were to go to the pond, Thornton insisted upon our repairing there to avoid suspicion."

Dawson then proceeded to say, that, on their return, as he was still exceedingly nervous, Thornton insisted on his going to bed. When our party from Lord Chester's came to the house, Thornton went into Dawson's room, and made him swallow a large tumbler of brandy; [Note: A common practice with thieves, who fear the weak nerves of their accomplices.] this intoxicated him so as to make him less sensible to his dangerous situation. Afterwards, when the picture was found, which circumstance Thornton communicated to him, along with that of the threatening letter sent by Glanville to the deceased, which was discovered in Tyrrell's pocket-book, Dawson recovered courage; and justice being entirely thrown on a wrong scent, he managed to pass his examination without suspicion. He then went to town with Thornton, and constantly attended "the club" to which Jonson had before introduced him; at first, among his new comrades, and while the novel flush of the money, he had so fearfully acquired, lasted, he partially succeeded in stifling his remorse. But the success of crime is too contrary to nature to continue long; his poor wife, whom, in spite of her extravagant, and his dissolute habits, he seemed really to love, fell ill, and died; on her deathbed she revealed the suspicions she had formed of his crime, and said, that those suspicions had preyed upon, and finally destroyed her health; this awoke him from the guilty torpor of his conscience. His share of the money, too, the greater part of which Thornton had bullied out of him, was gone. He fell, as Job had said, into despondency and gloom, and often spoke to Thornton so forcibly of his remorse, and so earnestly of his gnawing and restless desire to appease his mind, by surrendering himself to justice, that the fears of that villain grew, at length, so thoroughly alarmed, as to procure his removal to his present abode.

It was here that his real punishment commenced; closely confined to his apartment, at the remotest corner of the house, his solitude was never broken but by the short and hurried visits of his female gaoler, and (worse even than loneliness), the occasional invasions of Thornton. There appeared to be in that abandoned wretch what, for the honour of human nature, is but rarely found, viz., a love of sin, not for its objects, but itself. With a malignity, doubly fiendish from its inutility, he forbade Dawson the only indulgence he craved—a light, during the dark hours; and not only insulted him for his cowardice, but even added to his terrors, by threats of effectually silencing them.

These fears had so wildly worked upon the man's mind, that prison itself appeared to him an elysium to the hell he endured; and when his confession was ended, I said, "If you can be freed from this place, would you repeat before a magistrate all that you have now told me?"

He started up in delight at the very thought; in truth, besides his remorse, and that inward and impelling voice which, in all the annals of murder, seems to urge the criminal onwards to the last expiation of his guilt—besides these, there mingled in his mind a sentiment of bitter, yet cowardly, vengeance, against his inhuman accomplice; and perhaps he found consolation for his own fate, in the hope of wreaking upon Thornton's head somewhat of the tortures that ruffian had inflicted upon him.

I had taken down in my book the heads of the confession, and I now hastened to Jonson, who, waiting without the door, had (as I had anticipated) heard all.

"You see," said I, "that, however satisfactory this recital has been, it contains no secondary or innate proofs to confirm it; the only evidence with which it could furnish us, would be the remnant of the broken knife, engraved with Thornton's name; but you have heard from Dawson's account, how impossible it would be in an extensive wood, for any to discover the spot but himself. You will agree with me, therefore, that we must not leave this house without Dawson."

Job changed colour slightly.

"I see as clearly as you do," said he, "that it will be necessary for my annuity, and your friend's full acquittal, to procure Dawson's personal evidence, but it is late now; the men may be still drinking below; Bess may be still awake, and stirring; even if she sleeps, how could we pass her room without disturbing her? I own that I do not see a chance of effecting his escape to-night, without incurring the most probable peril of having our throats cut. Leave it, therefore, to me to procure his release as soon as possible—probably to-morrow, and let us now quietly retire, content with what we have yet got."

Hitherto I had implicitly obeyed Job; it was now my turn to command. "Look you," said I, calmly, but sternly, "I have come into this house under your guidance solely, to procure the evidence of that man; the evidence he has, as yet, given may not be worth a straw; and, since I have ventured among the knives of your associates, it shall be for some purpose. I tell you fairly that, whether you befriend or betray me, I will either leave these walls with Dawson, or remain in them a corpse."

"You are a bold blade, Sir," said Jonson, who seemed rather to respect than resent the determination of my tone, "and we will see what can be done: wait here, your honour, while I go down to see if the boys are gone to bed, and the coast is clear."

Job descended, and I re-entered Dawson's room. When I told him that we were resolved, if possible, to effect his escape, nothing could exceed his transport and gratitude; this was, indeed, expressed in so mean and servile a manner, mixed with so many petty threats of vengeance against Thornton, that I could scarcely conceal my disgust.

Jonson returned, and beckoned me out of the room.

"They are all in bed, Sir," said he—"Bess as well as the rest; indeed, the old girl has lushed so well at the bingo, that she sleeps as if her next morrow was the day of judgment. I have, also, seen that the street door is still unbarred, so that, upon the whole, we have, perhaps, as good a chance to-night as we may ever have again. All my fear is about that cowardly lubber. I have left both Bess's doors wide open, so we have nothing to do but to creep through; as for me, I am an old file, and could steal my way through a sick man's room, like a sunbeam through a keyhole."

"Well," said I, in the same strain, "I am no elephant, and my dancing master used to tell me I might tread on a butterfly's wing without brushing off a tint: poor Coulon! he little thought of the use his lessons would be to me hereafter!—so let us be quick, Master Job."

"Stop," said Jonson; "I have yet a ceremony to perform with our caged bird. I must put a fresh gag on his mouth; for though, if he escapes, I must leave England, perhaps, for ever, for fear of the jolly boys, and, therefore, care not what he blabs about me; yet there are a few fine fellows amongst the club whom I would not have hurt for the Indies; so I shall make Master Dawson take our last oath—the Devil himself would not break that, I think! Your honour will stay outside the door, for we can have no witness while it is administered."

Job then entered; I stood without;—in a few minutes I heard Dawson's voice in the accents of supplication. Soon after Job returned, "The craven dog won't take the oath," said he, "and may my right hand rot above ground before it shall turn key for him unless he does." But when Dawson saw that Job had left the room, and withdrawn the light, the conscience-stricken coward came to the door, and implored Job to return. "Will you swear then?" said Jonson; "I will, I will," was the answer.

Job then re-entered—minutes passed away—Job re-appeared, and Dawson was dressed, and clinging hold of him—"All's right," said he to me, with a satisfied air.

The oath had been taken—what it was I know not—but it was never broken. [Note: Those conversant with the annals of Newgate, will know how religiously the oaths of these fearful Freemasonries are kept.]

Dawson and Job went first—I followed—we passed the passage, and came to the chamber of the sleeping Mrs. Brimstone. Job leant eagerly forward to listen, before we entered; he took hold of Dawson's arm, and beckoning to me to follow, stole, with a step that a blind mole would not have heard, across the room. Carefully did the practised thief veil the candle he carried, with his hand, as he now began to pass by the bed. I saw that Dawson trembled like a leaf, and the palpitation of his limbs made his step audible and heavy. Just as they had half-way passed the bed, I turned my look on Brimstone Bess, and observed, with a shuddering thrill, her eyes slowly open, and fix upon the forms of my companions. Dawson's gaze had been bent in the same direction, and when he met the full, glassy stare of the beldame's eyes, he uttered a faint scream. This completed our danger; had it not been for that exclamation, Bess might, in the uncertain vision of drowsiness, have passed over the third person, and fancied it was only myself and Jonson, in our way from Dawson's apartment; but no sooner had her ear caught the sound, than she started up, and sat erect on her bed, gazing at us in mingled wrath and astonishment.

That was a fearful moment—we stood rivetted to the spot! "Oh, my kiddies," cried Bess, at last finding speech, "you are in Queer-street, I trow! Plant your stumps, Master Guinea Pig; you are going to stall off the Daw's baby in prime twig, eh? But Bess stags you, my cove! Bess stags you."

Jonson, looked irresolute for one instant; but the next he had decided. "Run, run," cried he, for your lives," and he and Dawson (to whom, fear did indeed lend wings) were out of the room in an instant. I lost no time in following their example; but the vigilant and incensed hag was too quick for me; she pulled violently the bell, on which she had already placed her hand: the alarm rang like an echo in a cavern; below—around— far—near—from wall to wall—from chamber to chamber, the sound seemed multiplied and repeated! and in the same breathing point of time, she sprang from her bed, and seized me, just as I had reached the door.

"On, on, on," cried Jonson's voice to Dawson, as they had already gained the passage, and left the whole room, and the staircase beyond, in utter darkness.

With a firm, muscular, nervous gripe, which almost shewed a masculine strength, the hag clung to my throat and breast; behind, among some of the numerous rooms in the passage we had left, I heard sounds, which told too plainly how rapidly the alarm had spread. A door opened—steps approached—my fate seemed fixed; but despair gave me energy: it was no time for the ceremonials due to the beau sexe. I dashed Bess to the ground, tore myself from her relaxing grasp, and fled down the steps with all the precipitation the darkness would allow. I gained the passage, at the far end of which hung the lamp, now weak and waning in its socket; which, it will be remembered, burnt close by the sick man's chamber that I had so unintentionally entered. A thought flashed upon my mind, and lent me new nerves and fresh speed; I flew along the passage, guided by the dying light. The staircase I had left, shook with the footsteps of my pursuers. I was at the door of the sick thief—I burst it open—seized the sword as it lay within reach on the chair, where Jonson had placed it, and feeling, at the touch of the familiar weapon, as if the might of ten men had been transferred to my single arm, I bounded down the stairs before me — passed the door at the bottom, which Dawson had fortunately left open — flung it back almost upon the face of my advancing enemies, and found myself in the long passage which led to the street-door, in safety, but in the thickest darkness. A light flashed from a door to the left; the door was that of the "Common Room" which we had first entered; it opened, and Spider-shanks, with one of his comrades, looked forth; the former holding a light. I darted by them, and, guided by their lamp, fled along the passage, and reached the door. Imagine my dismay! when, either through accident, or by the desire of my fugitive companions to impede pursuit, I found it unexpectedly closed.

The two villains had now come up to me, close at their heels were two more, probably my pursuers, from the upper apartments. Providentially the passage was (as I before said) extremely narrow, and as long as no fire- arms were used, nor a general rush resorted to, I had little doubt of being able to keep the ruffians at bay, until I had hit upon the method of springing the latch, and so winning my escape from the house.

While my left hand was employed in feeling the latch, I made such good use of my right, as to keep my antagonists at a safe distance. The one who was nearest to me, was Fib Fakescrew; he was armed with a weapon exactly similar to my own. the whole passage rung with oaths and threats. "Crash the cull — down with him — down with him, before he dubs the jigger. Tip him the degen, Fib, fake him through and through; if he pikes, we shall all be scragged."

Hitherto, in the confusion I had not been able to recall Job's instructions in opening the latch; at last I remembered, and pressed, the screw — the latch rose — I opened the door; but not wide enough to scape through the aperture. The ruffians saw my escape at hand. "Rush the b— cove! rush him!" cried the loud voice of one behind; and at the word, Fib was thrown forwards upon the extended edge of my blade; scarcely with an effort of my own arm, the sword entered his bosom, and he fell at my feet bathed in blood; the motion which the men thought would prove my destruction, became my salvation; staggered by the fall of their companion they gave way: I seized advantage of the momentary confusion — threw open the door, and, mindful of Job's admonition, turned to the right, and fled onwards, with a rapidity which baffled and mocked pursuit.

CHAPTER LXXXIV.

Ille viam secat ad naves sociosque, revisit.
       —Virgil.

The day had already dawned, but all was still and silent; my footsteps smote the solitary pavement with a strange and unanswered sound. Nevertheless, though all pursuit had long ceased, I still continued to run on mechanically, till, faint and breathless, I was forced into pausing. I looked round, but could recognize nothing familiar in the narrow and filthy streets; even the names of them were to me like an unknown language. After a brief rest I renewed my wanderings, and at length came to an alley, called River Lane; the name did not deceive me, but brought me, after a short walk, to the Thames; there, to my inexpressible joy, I discovered a solitary boatman, and transported myself forthwith to the Whitehall-stairs.

Never, I ween, did gay gallant, in the decaying part of the season, arrive at those stairs for the sweet purpose of accompanying his own mistress, or another's wife, to green Richmond, or sunny Hampton, with more eager and animated delight than I felt at rejecting the arm of the rough boatman, and leaping on the well-known stones. I hastened to that stand of "jarvies" which has often been the hope and shelter of belated member of St. Stephen's, or bewetted fugitive from the Opera. I startled a sleeping coachman, flung myself into his vehicle, and descended at Mivart's.

The drowsy porter surveyed, and told me to be gone; I had forgotten my strange attire. "Pooh, my friend," said I, "may not Mr. Pelham go to a masquerade as well as his betters?" My voice and words undeceived my Cerberus, and I was admitted; I hastened to bed, and no sooner had I laid my head on my pillow, than I fell fast asleep. It must be confessed, that I had deserved "tired Nature's sweet restorer."

I had not been above a couple of hours in the land of dreams, when I was awakened by some one grasping my arm; the events of the past night were so fresh in my memory, that I sprung up, as if the knife was at my throat—my eyes opened upon the peaceful countenance of Mr. Job Jonson.

"Thank Heaven, Sir, you are safe! I had but a very faint hope of finding you here when I came."

"Why," said I, rubbing my eyes, "it is very true that I am safe, honest Job: but, I believe, I have few thanks to give you for a circumstance so peculiarly agreeable to myself. It would have saved me much trouble, and your worthy friend, Mr. Fib Fakescrew, some pain, if you had left the door open instead of shutting me up with your club, as you are pleased to call it."

"Very true, Sir," said Job, "and I am extremely sorry at the accident; it was Dawson who shut the door, through utter unconsciousness, though I told him especially not to do it—the poor dog did not know whether he was on his head or his heels."

"You have got him safe," said I, quickly.

"Aye, trust me for that, your honour. I have locked him up at home while
I came here to look for you."

"We will lose no time in transferring him to safer custody," said I, leaping out of bed; "but be off to—Street directly."

"Slow and sure, Sir," answered Jonson. "It is for you to do whatever you please, but my part of the business is over. I shall sleep at Dover tonight, and breakfast at Calais to-morrow. Perhaps it will not be very inconvenient to your honour to furnish me with my first quarter's annuity in advance, and to see that the rest is duly paid into Lafitte's, at Paris, for the use of Captain Douglas. Where I shall live hereafter is at present uncertain; but I dare say there will be few corners except old England and new England, in which I shall not make merry on your honour's bounty."

"Pooh! my good fellow," rejoined I, "never desert a country to which your talents do such credit; stay here, and reform on your annuity. If ever I can accomplish my own wishes, I will consult your's still farther; for I shall always think of your services with gratitude, though you did shut the door in my face."

"No, Sir," replied Job—"life is a blessing I would fain enjoy a few years longer; and, at present, my sojourn in England would put it woefully in danger of 'club law.' Besides, I begin to think that a good character is a very agreeable thing, when not too troublesome: and, as I have none left in England, I may as well make the experiment abroad. If your honour will call at the magistrate's, and take a warrant and an officer, for the purpose of ridding me of my charge, at the very instant I see my responsibility at an end, I will have the honour of bidding you adieu."

"Well, as you please," said I. "Curse your scoundrel's cosmetics! How the deuce am I ever to regain my natural complexion? Look ye, sirrah! you have painted me with a long wrinkle on the left side of my mouth, big enough to engulph all the beauty I ever had. Why, water seems to have no effect upon it!"

"To be sure not, Sir," said Job, calmly—"I should be but a poor dauber, if my paints washed off with a wet sponge."

"Grant me patience," cried I, in a real panic; "how, in the name of Heaven, are they to wash off? Am I, before I have reached my twenty- third year, to look like a methodist parson on the wrong side of forty, you rascal!"

"The latter question, your honour can best answer," returned Job. "With regard to the former, I have an unguent here, if you will suffer me to apply it, which will remove all other colours than those which nature has bestowed upon you."

With that, Job produced a small box; and, after a brief submission to his skill, I had the ineffable joy of beholding myself restored to my original state. Nevertheless, my delight was somewhat checked by the loss of my ringlets: I thanked Heaven, however, that the damage had been sustained after Ellen's acceptation of my addresses. A lover confined to one, should not be too destructive, for fear of the consequences to the remainder of the female world: compassion is ever due to the fair sex.

My toilet being concluded, Jonson and I repaired to the magistrate's. He waited at the corner of the street, while I entered the
house —

       "'Twere vain to tell what shook the holy man,
       Who looked, not lovingly, at that divan."

Having summoned to my aid the redoubted Mr. _____, of mul-
berry-cheeked recollection, we entered a hackney-coach, and drove
to Jonson's lodgings, Job mounting guard on the box.

"I think, Sir," said Mr. _____, looking up at the man of two virtues,
"that I have had the pleasure of seeing that gentleman before."

"Very likely," said I; "he is a young man greatly about town."

When we had safely lodged Dawson (who seemed more collec-
ted, and even courageous, than I had expected) in the coach, Job
beckoned me into a little parlour. I signed him a draught on my
bankers for one hundred pounds—though at that time it was like
letting the last drop from my veins—and faithfully promised,
should Dawson's evidence procure the desired end (of which, indeed, there was now no doubt), that the annuity should be regularly
paid, as he desired. We then took an affectionate farewell of each
other.

"Adieu, Sir!" said Job, "I depart into a new world—that of honest
men!"

"If so," said I, "adieu, indeed!—for on this earth we shall never
meet again!"

We returned to—Street. As I was descending from the coach, a
female, wrapped from head to foot in a cloak, came eagerly up to
me, and seized me by the arm. "For God's sake," said she, in a low,
hurried voice, "come aside, and speak to me for a single moment."
Consigning Dawson to the sole charge of the officer, I did as I was
desired. When we had got some paces down the street, the female
stopped. Though she held her veil closely drawn over her face, her
voice and air were not to be mistaken: I knew her at once. "Glanville," said she, with great agitation, "Sir Reginald Glanville! tell me, is
he in real danger?" She stopped short— she could say no more.

"I trust not!" said I, appearing not to recognize the speaker.

"I trust not!" she repeated, "is that all!" And then the passionate feelings of her sex overcoming every other consideration, she seized me by the hand, and said—"Oh, Mr. Pelham, for mercy's sake, tell me is he in the power of that villain Thornton? you need disguise nothing from me, I know all the fatal history."

"Compose yourself, dear, dear Lady Roseville," said I, soothingly; "for it is in vain any longer to affect not to know you. Glanville is safe; I have brought with me a witness whose testimony must release him."

"God bless you, God bless you!" said Lady Roseville, and she burst into tears; but she dried them directly, and recovering some portion of that dignity which never long forsakes a woman of virtuous and educated mind, she resumed, proudly, yet bitterly—"It is no ordinary motive, no motive which you might reasonably impute to me, that has brought me here. Sir Reginald Glanville can never be any thing more to me than a friend—but of all friends, the most known and valued. I learned from his servant of his disappearance; and my acquaintance with his secret history enabled me to account for it in the most fearful manner. In short I—I—but explanations are idle now; you will never say that you have seen me here, Mr. Pelham: you will endeavour even to forget it—farewell."

Lady Roseville, then drawing her cloak closely round her, left me with a fleet and light step, and turning the corner of the street, disappeared.

I returned to my charge, I demanded an immediate interview with the magistrate. "I have come," said I, "to redeem my pledge, and acquit the innocent." I then briefly related my adventures, only concealing (according to my promise) all description of my helpmate, Job; and prepared the worthy magistrate for the confession and testimony of Dawson. That unhappy man had just concluded his narration, when an officer entered, and whispered the magistrate that Thornton was in waiting.

"Admit him," said Mr. _____, aloud. Thornton entered with his usual easy and swaggering air of effrontery; but no sooner did he set his eyes upon Dawson, than a deadly and withering change passed over his countenance. Dawson could not bridle the cowardly petulance of his spite—"They know all, Thornton!" said he, with a look of triumph. The villain turned slowly from him to us, muttering something we could not hear. He saw upon my face, upon the magistrate's, that his doom was sealed; his desperation gave him presence of mind, and he made a sudden rush to the door; the officers in waiting seized him. Why should I detail the rest of the scene? He was that day fully committed for trial, and Sir Reginald Glanville honourably released, and unhesitatingly acquitted.

CHAPTER LXXXV.

The main interest of my adventures — if, indeed, I may flatter myself that they ever contained any — is now over; the mystery is explained, the innocent acquitted, and the guilty condemned. Moreover, all obstacles between the marriage of the unworthy hero, with the peerless heroine, being removed, it would be but an idle prolixity to linger over the preliminary details of an orthodox and customary courtship. Nor is it for me to dilate upon the exaggerated expressions of gratitude, in which the affectionate heart of Glanville found vent for my fortunate exertions on his behalf. He was not willing that any praise to which I might be entitled for them, should be lost. He narrated to Lady Glanville and Ellen my adventures with the comrades of the worthy Job; from the lips of the mother, and the eyes of the dear sister, came my sweetest addition to the good fortune which had made me the instrument of Glanville's safety, and acquittal. I was not condemned to a long protraction of that time, which, if it be justly termed the happiest of our lives, we, (viz. all true lovers) through that perversity common to human nature, most ardently wish to terminate.

On that day month which saw Glanville's release, my bridals were appointed. Reginald was even more eager than myself in pressing for an early day: firmly persuaded that his end was rapidly approaching, his most prevailing desire was to witness our union. This wish, and the interest he took in our happiness, gave him an energy and animation which impressed us with the deepest hopes for his ultimate recovery; and the fatal disease to which he was a prey, nursed the fondness of our hearts by the bloom of cheek, and brightness of eye, with which it veiled its desolating and gathering progress.

From the eventful day on which I had seen Lady Roseville, in — Street, we had not met. She had shut herself up in her splendid home, and the newspapers teemed with regret, at the reported illness and certain seclusion of one, whose fetes and gaieties had furnished them with their brightest pages. The only one admitted to her was Ellen. To her, she had for some time made no secret of her attachment — and of her the daily news of Sir Reginald's health was ascertained. Several times, when at a late hour, I left Glanville's apartments, I passed the figure of a woman, closely muffled, and apparently watching before his windows — which, owing to the advance of summer, were never closed — to catch, perhaps, a view of his room, or a passing glimpse of his emaciated and fading figure. If that sad and lonely vigil was kept by her whom I suspected, deep, indeed, and mighty, was the love, which could so humble the heart, and possess the spirit, of the haughty and high-born Countess of Roseville.

I turn to a very different personage in this veritable histoire. My father and mother were absent, at Lady H.'s, when my marriage was fixed; to both of them I wrote for their approbation of my choice. From Lady Frances I received the answer which I subjoin: —

"My dearest Son,

"Your father desires me to add his congratulations to mine, upon the election you have made. I shall hasten to London, to be present at the ceremony. Although you must not be offended with me, if I say, that with your person, accomplishments, birth, and (above all) high ton, you might have chosen among the loftiest, and wealthiest families in the country, yet I am by no means displeased or disappointed with your future wife, to say nothing of the antiquity of her name. (The Glanvilles intermarried with the Pelhams, in the reign of Henry II.) It is a great step to future distinction to marry a beauty, especially one so celebrated as Miss Glanville — perhaps it is among the surest ways to the cabinet. The forty thousand pounds which you say Miss Glanville is to receive, makes, to be sure, but a slender income; though, when added to your own, it would have been a great addition to the Glenmorris property, if your uncle — I have no patience with him — had not married again.

"However, you will lose no time in getting into the House — at all events, the capital will ensure your return for a borough, and maintain you comfortably, till you are in the administration; when of course it matters very little what your fortune may be — tradesmen will be too happy to have your name in their books; be sure, therefore, that the money is not tied up. Miss Glanville must see that her

own interest, as well as yours, is concerned in your having the un-
fettered disposal of a fortune, which, if restricted, you would find it
impossible to live upon. Pray, how is Sir Reginald Glanville? Is his
cough as bad as ever? He has no entailed property, I think?

"Will you order Stonor to have the house ready for us on Friday,
when I shall return home in time for dinner? Let me again congratulate you, most sincerely, on your choice. I always thought you had
more common sense, as well as genius, than any young man, I ever
knew: you have shown it in this important step. Domestic happiness, my dearest Henry, ought to be peculiarly sought for by every
Englishman, however elevated his station; and when I reflect upon
Miss Glanville's qualifications, and her renommee as a belle ce-
lebree, I have no doubt of your possessing the felicity you deserve.
But be sure that the fortune is not settled away from you; poor Sir
Reginald is not (I believe) at all covetous or worldly, and will not
therefore insist upon the point.

"God bless you, and grant you every happiness.

"Ever, my dear Henry,
"Your very affectionate Mother,

"F. Pelham."

"P.S. I think it will be better to give out that Miss Glanville has
eighty thousand pounds. Be sure, therefore, that you do not contra-
dict me."

The days, the weeks flew away. Ah, happy days! yet, I do not regret while I recal you! He that loves much, fears even in his best
founded hopes. What were the anxious longings for a treasure — in
my view only, not in my possession — to the deep joy of finding it
for ever my own! The day arrived — I was yet at my toilet, and Bedos, in the greatest confusion (poor fellow, he was as happy as myself), when a letter was brought me, stamped with the foreign post-
mark. It was from the exemplary Job Jonson; and though I did not
even open it on that day, yet it shall be more favoured by the reader — viz. if he will not pass over, without reading, the following
effusion —

"Rue des Moulins, No.__, Paris.

"Honoured Sir,

"I arrived in Paris safely, and reading in the English papers the full success of our enterprise, as well as in the Morning Post of the __th, your approaching marriage with Miss Glanville, I cannot refrain from the liberty of congratulating you upon both, as well as of reminding you of the exact day on which the first quarter of my annuity will be paid—it is the—of—; for, I presume, your honour kindly made me a present of the draft for one hundred pounds, in order to pay my travelling expenses.

"I find that the boys are greatly incensed against me; but as Dawson was too much bound by his oath, to betray a tittle against them, I trust I shall, ultimately, pacify the club, and return to England. A true patriot, Sir, never loves to leave his native country. Even were I compelled to visit Van Diemen's land, the ties of birthplace would be so strong as to induce me to seize the first opportunity of returning. I am not, your honour, very fond of the French—they are an idle, frivolous, penurious, poor nation. Only think, Sir, the other day I saw a gentleman of the most noble air secrete something at a cafe, which could not clearly discern; as he wrapped it carefully in paper, before he placed it in his pocket, I judged that it was a silver cream ewer, at least; accordingly, I followed him out, and from pure curiosity—I do assure your honour, it was from no other motive—I transferred this purloined treasure to my own pocket. You will imagine, Sir, the interest with which I hastened to a lonely spot in the Tuileries, and carefully taking out the little packet, unfolded paper by paper, till I came—yes, Sir, till I came to—five lumps of sugar! Oh, the French are a mean people—a very mean people—I hope I shall soon be able to return to England. Meanwhile, I am going into Holland, to see how those rich burghers spend their time and their money. I suppose poor Dawson, as well as the rascal Thornton, will be hung before you receive this—they deserve it richly—it is such fellows who disgrace the profession. He is but a very poor bungler who is forced to cut throats as well as pockets. And now, your honour, wishing you all happiness with your lady,

"I beg to remain,
"Your very obedient humble Servant,

    "Ferdinand De Courcy, etc."

Struck with the joyous countenance of my honest valet, as I took my gloves and hat from his hand, I could not help wishing to bestow upon him a similar blessing to that I was about to possess. "Bedos," said I, "Bedos, my good fellow, you left your wife to come to me; you shall not suffer by your fidelity: send for her—we will find room for her in our future establishment."

The smiling face of the Frenchman underwent a rapid change. "Ma foi," said he, in his own tongue; "Monsieur is too good. An excess of happiness hardens the heart; and so, for fear of forgetting my gratitude to Providence, I will, with Monsieur's permission, suffer my adored wife to remain where she is."

After so pious a reply, I should have been worse than wicked had I pressed the matter any farther.

I found all ready at Berkeley-square. Lady Glanville is one of those good persons, who think a marriage out of church is no marriage at all; to church, therefore, we went. Although Sir Reginald was now so reduced that he could scarcely support the least fatigue, he insisted on giving Ellen away. He was that morning, and had been, for the last two or three days, considerably better, and our happiness seemed to grow less selfish in our increasing hope of his recovery.

When we returned from church, our intention was to set off immediately to—Hall, a seat which I had hired for our reception. On re-entering the house, Glanville called me aside—I followed his infirm and tremulous steps into a private apartment.

"Pelham," said he, "we shall never meet again! no matter—you are now happy, and I shall shortly be so. But there is one office I have yet to request from your friendship; when I am dead, let me be buried by her side, and let one tombstone cover both."

I pressed his hand, and, with tears in my eyes, made him the promise he required.

"It is enough," said he; "I have no farther business with life. God bless you, my friend — my brother; do not let a thought of me cloud your happiness."

He rose, and we turned to quit the room; Glanville was leaning on my arm; when we had moved a few paces towards the door, he stopped abruptly. Imagining that the pause proceeded from pain or debility, I turned my eyes upon his countenance — a fearful and convulsive change was rapidly passing over it — his eyes stared wildly upon vacancy.

"Merciful God — is it — can it be?" he said, in a low inward tone. At that moment, I solemnly declare, whether from my sympathy with his feelings, or from some more mysterious and undefinable cause, my whole frame shuddered from limb to limb. I saw nothing — I heard nothing; but I felt, as it were, within me some awful and ghostly presence, which had power to curdle my blood into ice, and cramp my sinews into impotence; it was as if some preternatural and shadowy object darkened across the mirror of my soul — as if, without the medium of the corporeal senses, a spirit spake to, and was answered by, a spirit.

The moment was over. I felt Glanville's hand relax its grasp upon my arm- -he fell upon the floor — I raised him — a smile of ineffable serenity and peace was upon his lips; his face was as the face of an angel, but the spirit had passed away!

CHAPTER LXXXVI.

> Now haveth good day, good men all,
> Haveth good day, young and old;
> Haveth good day, both great and small,
> And graunt merci a thousand fold!
> Gif ever I might full fain I wold,
> Don ought that were unto your leve
> Christ keep you out of cares cold,
> For now 'tis time to take my leave.
> —Old Song.

Several months have now elapsed since my marriage. I am living quietly in the country, among my books, and looking forward with calmness, rather than impatience, to the time which shall again bring me before the world. Marriage with me is not that sepulchre of all human hope and energy which it often is with others. I am not more partial to my arm chair, nor more averse to shaving, than of yore. I do not bound my prospects to the dinner-hour, nor my projects to "migrations from the blue bed to the brown." Matrimony found me ambitious; it has not cured me of the passion: but it has concentrated what was scattered, and determined what was vague. If I am less anxious than formerly for the reputation to be acquired in society, I am more eager for honour in the world; and instead of amusing my enemies, and the saloon, I trust yet to be useful to my friends and to mankind.

Whether this is a hope, altogether vain and idle; whether I have, in the self-conceit common to all men, peculiarly prominent in myself, overrated both the power and the integrity of my mind (for the one is bootless without the other,) neither I nor the world can yet tell. "Time," says one of the fathers, "is the only touchstone which distinguishes the prophet from the boaster."

Meanwhile, gentle reader, during the two years which I purpose devoting to solitude and study, I shall not be so occupied with my fields and folios, as to render me uncourteous to thee. If ever thou hast known me in the city, I give thee a hearty invitation to come and visit me in the country. I promise thee, that my wines and viands shall not disgrace the companion of Guloseton: nor my conversation be much duller than my book. I will compliment thee on thy horses, thou shalt congratulate me upon my wife. Over old wine we will talk over new events; and if we flag at the latter, why, we will make ourselves amends with the former. In short, if thou art neither very silly nor very wise, it shall be thine own fault if we are not excellent friends.

I feel that it would be but poor courtesy in me, after having kept company with Lord Vincent, through the tedious journey of three volumes, to dismiss him now without one word of valediction. May he, in the political course he has adopted, find all the admiration his talents deserve; and if ever we meet as foes, let our heaviest weapon be a quotation, and our bitterest vengeance a jest.

Lord Guloseton regularly corresponds with me, and his last letter contained a promise to visit me in the course of the month, in order to recover his appetite (which has been much relaxed of late) by the country air.

My uncle wrote to me, three weeks since, announcing the death of the infant Lady Glenmorris had brought him. Sincerely do I wish that his loss may be supplied. I have already sufficient fortune for my wants, and sufficient hope for my desires.

Thornton died as he had lived—the reprobate and the ruffian. "Pooh," said he, in his quaint brutality, to the worthy clergyman, who attended his last moments with more zeal than success; "Pooh, what's the difference between gospel and go—spell? we agree like a bell and its clapper—you're prating while I'm hanging."

Dawson died in prison, penitent and in peace. Cowardice, which spoils the honest man, often ameliorates the knave.

From Lord Dawton I have received a letter, requesting me to accept a borough (in his gift), just vacated. It is a pity that generosity—such a prodigal to those who do not want it—should often be such a niggard to those who do. I need not specify my answer. One may as well be free as dependant, when one can afford it; and I hope yet to teach Lord Dawton, that to forgive the minister is not to forget the affront. Meanwhile, I am content to bury myself in my retreat with my mute teachers of logic and legislature, in order, hereafter, to justify his lordship's good opinion of my senatorial abilities. Farewell, Brutus, we shall meet at Philippi!

It is some months since Lady Roseville left England; the last news we received of her, informed us, that she was living at Sienna, in utter seclusion, and very infirm health.

"The day drags thro', though storms keep out the sun,
And thus the heart will break, yet brokenly live on."

Poor Lady Glanville! the mother of one so beautiful, so gifted, and so lost. What can I say of her which "you, and you, and you—" all who are parents, cannot feel, a thousand times more acutely, in those recesses of the heart too deep for words or tears. There are yet many hours in which I find the sister of the departed in grief, that even her husband cannot console; and I—I—my friend, my brother, have I forgotten thee in death? I lay down the pen, I turn from my employment—thy dog is at my feet, and looking at me, as if conscious of my thoughts, with an eye almost as tearful as my own.

But it is not thus that I will part from my reader; our greeting was not in sorrow, neither shall be our adieus. For thee, who hast gone with me through the motley course of my confessions, I would fain trust that I have sometimes hinted at thy instruction when only appearing to strive for thy amusement. But on this I will not dwell; for the moral insisted upon often loses its effect, and all that I will venture to hope is, that I have opened to thee one true, and not utterly hacknied, page in the various and mighty volume of mankind. In this busy and restless world I have not been a vague speculator, nor an idle actor. While all around me were vigilant, I have not laid me down to sleep—even for the luxury of a poet's dream. Like the school boy, I have considered study as study, but action as delight.

Nevertheless, whatever I have seen, or heard, or felt, has been treasured
in my memory, and brooded over by my thoughts. I now place the result

before you,

> "Sicut meus est mos,
> Nescio quid meditans nugarum; —

but not, perhaps, — totus in illis."

Whatever society — whether in a higher or lower grade — I have portrayed, my sketches have been taken rather as a witness than a copyist; for I have never shunned that circle, nor that individual, which presented life in a fresh view, or man in a new relation. It is right, however, that I should add, that as I have not wished to be an individual satirist, rather than a general observer, I have occasionally, in the subordinate characters (such as Russelton and Gordon), taken only the outline from truth, and filled up the colours at my leisure and my will.

With regard to myself I have been more candid. I have not only shewn — non parca manu — my faults, but (grant that this is a much rarer exposure) my foibles; and, in my anxiety for your entertainment, I have not grudged you the pleasure of a laugh — even at my own expense. Forgive me, then, if I am not a fashionable hero — forgive me if I have not wept over a "blighted spirit," nor boasted of a "British heart;" and allow that, a man, who, in these days of alternate Werters and Worthies, is neither the one nor the other, is, at least, a novelty in print, though, I fear, common enough in life.

And, now my kind reader, having remembered the proverb, and in saying one word to thee, having said two for myself, I will no longer detain thee. Whatever thou mayest think of me and my thousand faults, both as an author, and a man, believe me it is with a sincere and affectionate wish for the accomplishment of my parting words, that I bid thee — FAREWELL!